Red Eyes
at Night

by Michael
Morpurgo

Illustrated by
Tony Ross

A
LITTLE APPLE
PAPERBACK

SCHOLASTIC INC.

New York Toronto London Auckland Sydney
Mexico City New Delhi Hong Kong Buenos Aires

For
Ted and Dorothy
and
their grandchildren

No part of this publication may be reproduced in whole or in part, or stored in a retrieval system, or transmitted in any form or by any means, electronic, mechanical, photocopying, or otherwise, without written permission of the publishers. For information regarding permission, write to Hodder Children's Books, A Division of Hodder Headline, 338 Euston Road, London NW1 3BH, United Kingdom.

ISBN 0-439-33475-6

Text copyright © 1998 by Michael Morpurgo
Illustrations copyright © 1998 by Tony Ross

All rights reserved. Published by Scholastic Inc., 555 Broadway, New York, NY 10012, by arrangement with Hodder Children's Books. SCHOLASTIC, LITTLE APPLE PAPERBACKS, and associated logos are trademarks and/or registered trademarks of Scholastic Inc.

12 11 10 9 8 7 6 5 4 3 2 1   1 2 3 4 5 6/0
                                              40

Printed in the U.S.A.
First Scholastic printing, September 2001

CONTENTS

CHAPTER ONE
Little Toad

My cousin Geraldine is a real little toad. Every summer it's the same — Geraldine comes to stay. And who has to look after her? I do, because there's no one else.

Dad's away all week. He always is. He's in pots and pans. "I'm in pots and pans." He's always saying that. It means he sells them — his little joke. Mom goes to work before breakfast every morning. She's a nurse. And that's another thing. It's no fun having a nurse for a mom. She always knows when I'm pretending to be sick when I'm not, like when I don't want to go to school.

That leaves just Gran and me, and Gran's got bad knees and can't walk around much. So *I* get stuck with Geraldine. I like to complain about it, just like I am now, but no one listens. "She'll be good company for you, Millie," Mom says. "Just look after her. And be nice."

Be nice! To Geraldine?!

Geraldine is only eight, two years younger than me, but you wouldn't know it. "Mature," Mom calls her. A stuck-up, hoity-toity little toad, that's what I call her.

She's so perfectly perfect — she always eats everything on her plate, brushes her teeth twice a day, makes her bed, does her hair, and she says please and thank you so often and so sweetly it makes you sick. What's worse is, she's so *good* at everything. She plays her cello so well you actually want to listen.

She can do ten cartwheels one after
the other, stand on her head for five
minutes at a time, and she can tap-
dance just like they do on Broadway.

I could put up with all that — just about — but when Geraldine comes to stay she sleeps in *my* bedroom, in *my* bed. (I have to sleep on a mattress on the floor.) She plays with *my* computer and reads *my* books — she never asks!

And, of course, she's got a *bigger* room than mine at home, a *miles* more up-to-date computer, and a *million* more books, she says.

But what really bugs me is Bingo. Bingo is my dog. I rescued him from the ASPCA. He's a mutt and the most adorable thing in the entire world. He's got eyes that melt your heart.

Normally, Bingo loves me and only me to pieces, but not when Geraldine's around. I don't know what it is about her, but he follows her everywhere. He sleeps with her on my bed. He even comes when she calls him. He brings balls back when she throws them for him. He never does that for me. There are times I would like to send Bingo back where he came from — and Geraldine could go with him, too.

CHAPTER TWO
The Real Jitters

So this summer, as usual, Geraldine shows up, parks her cello in the hallway, and makes herself at home right away. Bingo's all over her, and Gran's going on and on about how much she's grown up, how pretty she looks, and what a proper young lady she is.

Proper young lady.

Proper pain in the neck, if you ask me.

Anyway, there we are, the two of us, lying there in bed that first night, the rain lashing against the window, the thunder rumbling outside the house. Suddenly, Bingo starts whimpering in the darkness.

"What's the matter with him?" asks Geraldine.

"It's the thunder," I tell her. "He's scared of thunder. He always has been."

"Well, I'm not frightened of the thunder," she says.

White lightning fills the room, and then we're plunged back into pitch-darkness as the thunder crashes right overhead. Bingo's whimpering from under the bed now.

"Millie?" says Geraldine, sounding a little nervous.

"What?"

"I'm not scared of the dark, either, are you?"

"Of course not."

That's not true, of course, but she doesn't have to know that, does she?

"Me, neither," she says. "And anyway, where I live in the country, it's darker than it is here. And even then I'm not afraid, not ever. There's nothing to be scared of, is there?"

"Just the ghost," I tell her. I don't know why I said it. It just popped out. I didn't mean anything by it, not to begin with.

There's this long silence.

Then she tries to laugh it off.

But it's not a real laugh at all. I can

tell. She's scared! Geraldine's scared! And then, out of nowhere, I have this great idea. I'd seen it myself, when I was little, in Dad's shed, in the backyard. It gave me the real jitters, and if it gave me the jitters, then maybe . . .

"There are no such things as ghosts," she says. "Are there?"

"Of course there are," I whisper. "We've got one of our own. He's got red eyes that glow in the dark."

"Red eyes," she breathes. Now I've really got her going.

"Honest," I tell her. "He lives in Dad's shed — well, most of the time, anyway. He goes out at night, you know, like ghosts do, for a walk around."

"No, he doesn't!"

"I've seen him. I've seen him coming across the patio in the middle of the night, when everyone's gone to bed. And some nights, he even comes inside the house. He comes creeping up the stairs, along the landing. He turns the radio on. He leaves lights on. He switched on the television once. It's true. And he smells. He smells of pepper. I've smelled him. And wherever he goes, it's all cold and damp and shivery. I've felt him."

I'm doing well now, *really* well. The silence from her bed tells me so.

When she does speak, there's a wobble in her voice. "You're a liar, Millie," she says. "You're a horrible liar."

"I am not," I tell her.

Then the light goes on.

She's propped up on her elbows and as white as the sheets. "All right, prove it, then," she says. "Go on, prove it."

"If you like." I'm thinking now, thinking hard. I need time, time to

work things out, to arrange things, if you know what I mean. "Not tonight," I tell her. "It won't happen tonight. He never comes out if it's like this. Maybe he hates rain. Or maybe he doesn't like thunder, like Bingo. But tomorrow night should be okay, if the rain stops, that is." I turn over so she can't see me smiling.

"Better turn off the light," I say.

"You don't want to waste electricity. Unless you're frightened, of course."

"Of course I'm not. And anyway, I

don't believe you. So there. And you can't prove it. I know you can't."

"Nighty night." My voice is trilling now. "Nighty night. Don't let the vampires bite."

"Don't be so silly. It's not funny, you know."

"Oh, no, it's not funny," I tell her. "It's not funny at all," and I'm smothering my giggles as best I can. After a while I hear her lie down, but she doesn't turn off the light. The thunderstorm is moving away. There are ten seconds between the lightning and the thunder now, so it's ten miles away. She still hasn't turned off the light.

I'm lying there, trying to work out

how I'm going to fix up "the red-eyed ghost" for her. It wasn't going to be easy. I could do the pepper — that part would be simple enough, but as for the rest . . . Then I start drifting off to sleep. I can't help myself.

When I wake up the next morning, the light's still on, Geraldine's fast asleep with her thumb in her mouth, and Bingo's stretched out beside her, his nose in her ear. I still haven't worked it all out, about "the red-eyed ghost." But sometimes you get lucky. The thing about luck is that you never know where it's coming from, or when it's coming, either.

CHAPTER THREE
A Lot of Old Hogwash

So there we are at breakfast, just Gran
and Geraldine and Bingo and me.
Gran's going on about lightning and
how you shouldn't stand under trees
in a thunderstorm or use the phone. "I
got struck once," she says. "While I
was on the phone. It threw me clear
across the room. It was dreadful. I had
a ringing in my head for a week."

Then I notice Geraldine, and so
does Gran. She's not
eating her cornflakes.
She hasn't touched

her toast, either. She's just sitting there, looking all sad and thoughtful and sorry for herself. Bingo knows it, too. He's got his head on her lap, his eyes looking up at her all lovey-dovey and adoring. Mangy mutt!

"Is anything the matter, dear?" Gran asks her as she pours some coffee. "You don't look like yourself. Didn't you sleep well? Did the thunder keep you awake?"

"Gran?" Geraldine's up to something. I can hear it in her voice. "Gran? Do you believe in ghosts?" She's going to get me in trouble. Little toad.

Gran starts laughing. "Ghosts? Of course not. Of course I don't. Hogwash, a lot of old hogwash, that's what ghosts are. I believe in what I can see, nothing else. There's no such things as ghosts, except in stories, of course."

Geraldine's smiling at me across the table, her sickening told-you-so kind of smile.

"But Gran," she says, and she's still looking at me, still smiling, "just suppose there were ghosts — which there aren't, of course — but just suppose, they wouldn't have red eyes, would they? And they wouldn't smell of pepper, would they?"

"Red eyes? Pepper?" says Gran. "What is the matter with you this morning, Geraldine? What's this all about? Ghosts that smell of pepper! Red eyes! Hogwash! Hogwash! No more of this nonsense! Eat your cornflakes now, dear."

Before you can say "cornflakes," Geraldine has scoffed down her cereal *and* three pieces of toast, *and* she's feeding Bingo the crusts.

(Gran sees her doing it and she never says a thing!) I always have to eat my crusts, and I'm never allowed to feed Bingo from the table, either.

What's even worse is, whenever Gran's not looking, Geraldine's sticking her thumbs in her ears and wriggling her fingers at me. And do you know what she gets? I'll tell you.

She gets a "good girl" from Gran for eating her cornflakes, *and* a kiss

on the head when she offers to help
wash the breakfast dishes.

So that's how I come to find myself
doing the drying, with Gran going in
and out of the kitchen and Bingo
eating the crusts under the breakfast
table. And every time Gran goes out,
Geraldine flicks soapsuds in my face.
There's nothing I can do about it, not
with Gran coming back in again. For
the moment, I just have to grin and
bear it. But not for long. Oh, no, not
for long.

CHAPTER FOUR
Cat on a Hot Tin Roof

After breakfast, we're outside playing
in the backyard. Geraldine does
amazing things on the swing set. She's
hanging by her toes, like a bat, when
Bingo sees the cat next door. That
cat's always sunning himself on the tin
roof of Dad's shed, and Bingo does not
like it — not one bit. Suddenly, he's
running across the grass and
starts barking like crazy.

The cat's vanished
already, but Bingo
likes to make

sure he doesn't come back. So he's standing by the shed telling the cat just what he thinks of him.

"What's the matter with Bingo?" says upside-down Geraldine.

"It's the shed. He doesn't like it, not since *he*

moved in. Dogs can sense things, you know."

"Yeah, yeah," she says sarcastically. But then she swings herself upright, and I notice she keeps glancing at the shed and at Bingo, who's barking himself silly. And I know she's thinking about it. I know she's worried.

Later that same morning, we're down at the end of the yard, climbing the crab-apple tree. And, of course, Geraldine has to climb faster and higher than me. She's sitting up there on the branch above, swinging her legs and laughing at me loudly.

"Do you know, Millie, that you get spots on your tongue if you lie?" she's saying to me now. "I bet you've got millions on your tongue. And anyway, I never believed you. All about the red eyes and the pepper and stuff. I never believed you. Ghosts are stupid. He's not real, anyway. So there!"

I put my finger to my lips and point at the shed. "Shhh," I whisper. "You shouldn't. You *really* shouldn't."

"What do you mean?"

"You shouldn't talk about him. In case he's listening. He hates it when you talk about him. It makes him really angry. And when he's angry, oh, the things he does! It makes me shiver just to think about it."

"Oh, yeah." But then after a moment or two, she says, "What sort of things?"

"You know, ghostly sorts of things, *ghastly* sorts of things."

She's snorting at me now, pretending she

doesn't believe any
of it. But I know
better. So I go on. "He
rattles doors. He howls
around the house. He
leaves pools of blood on the
kitchen floor. And if he's really mad,
he comes up behind you and puts his
clammy hands around your throat.
Then he . . ."

"Stop," she's screaming at me now.
"I don't want to hear it. I don't want
to hear it." I look up. She's got her
hands over her ears. "I don't believe
it. I don't believe any of it."

"All right," I tell her, shrugging my
shoulders. "You asked. I was just
telling you, that's all. You believe
what you like. See if I care."

"It's not true, it can't be. Gran said

there's no such thing as ghosts! She said it was all hogwash!"

And then it comes to me, just like that, out of the blue. Call it intuition, call it inspiration, call it genius. Call it what you like. I'd worked it all out, the whole thing, in an instant.

"It's that word," I tell her, hushing my voice so I sound very mysterious.

"What word?"

"Hogwash. It's a sort of secret code, so we don't upset him. If anyone talks about him, if anyone even just says the word 'ghost,' one of us has to say 'hogwash.' Dad arranged it with him years ago. It means 'sorry.' But you can't go around saying 'sorry' to no one, can you? People would think we're all crazy, bonkers. So we say 'hogwash' instead. He hears us and he doesn't get angry. Didn't you notice how Gran kept saying it when you were asking about ghosts at breakfast? Hogwash. Hogwash. She kept saying it. Don't you remember?"

Suddenly, Geraldine's legs aren't swinging anymore. "But she said. Gran said. She said she didn't believe in . . . them. She told me they weren't real."

"Of course she did. She didn't want to scare you, that's all. But then, you're not scared of anything, are you? Not even ghosts." I clap my hand over my mouth. "Hogwash," I say, all muffled under my hand. "Hogwash. Hogwash. Hogwash."

Geraldine sits there for a moment or two in silence. I can *hear* her thinking. I really can. Bingo's stopped barking at last, and he's giving himself a good scratch behind the ear instead. Then, quick as a flash, she's down the tree and on the ground, looking very nervously at Dad's shed. "I'm feeling sick," she says. And goes running across the yard and around the goldfish pond toward the house, keeping herself well away from the shed, I notice.

I almost feel sorry for her, but only almost.

CHAPTER FIVE
Enough to Make You Sneeze

That evening we're all in the living room for Geraldine's cello concert, Mom, Gran, and me. Dad's still away, of course. When I say "concert," I really mean "practice." It's just Geraldine practicing, and for some reason I'm not quite sure of, we all have to sit there, listen, and clap, too. Normally, like I've said — and I don't like to say it — but *normally*, Geraldine's fantastic on her cello.

It makes me sick, she's so good. But not this evening. This evening, I'm glad to say, Geraldine's cello playing is definitely not what it should be. In

fact, it's horrible. Every note is like screeching chalk on a chalkboard. It's Bach, she says, but I can't quite believe it. Mom and Gran are giving

each other worried looks, and Bingo
has just crept out of the room with his
tail between his legs. Time for me to
go, too. I creep out, and as I go Mom
shoots me a look. "Bathroom," I
mouth to her, but I know she doesn't
believe me.

Bingo comes out into the backyard
with me. He's glad to get out, and I
don't blame him. It's cold out there
and I don't have much time, so I run.
Bingo disappears into the darkness, to
do his business, I expect.

Now, *no one* is ever allowed in

Dad's shed, unless he's there and unless he invites you. Gran calls it his "hideout," where he keeps his "toy" — that's what Mom calls it, anyway. They both tease him about it, but Dad doesn't care. He loves it in there. He spends hours fiddling with things. He's taken me in once or twice, but it was a long time ago, when I was little. To be honest, I found it all a bit boring, but I do know how to turn it on. Well, I think I do. I hope I do. And for what I've got in mind, that's all I'll need.

I fumble around in the darkness by the door of the shed for the conch shell where Dad hides the key. I let myself in. It's all musty in there, and I can't see a thing. I can't risk turning on the light, so I have to find it in the

dark, and that's not easy. Anyway,
after a little feeling around, I find
what I'm looking for and I turn it on.
I'm in and out of the shed in under a
minute.

All I need now is a little luck, the
most important ingredient of all —
and pepper, of course.

I creep back into the house and

tiptoe into the kitchen. The pepper shaker's just where it always is on the rack. It's the brown, dusty kind — it's better for sneezing. I pocket it quickly and then I go back to the living room for Geraldine's cello concert — which is still excruciating. Geraldine's looking really miserable. It's like she's fighting her cello, not playing it. I get a where-have-you-been look from Mom. I smile back at her sweetly, and at Geraldine, too. After all, I tell myself, I've got a lot to smile about. If all goes according to plan, and it should, then tonight's going to be special, *very* special.

CHAPTER SIX
My Grand Plan

Geraldine's mood is up and down like a
yo-yo. One minute she's down in the
dumps, the next she's happy as a clam.
I've given good-night hugs to Gran
and Mom, and I'm upstairs brushing
my teeth when Geraldine comes
breezing into the bathroom, all sparkly-
eyed and happy. I can't figure out why.
I don't have to ask. She soon tells me.

"I asked your mom," she says, squeezing out her toothpaste. I try not to look worried, but I am. She's grinning away as she brushes her teeth.

"So? What did you ask her?" I say.

"What do you think? About your silly red-eyed ghost that smells of pepper, that's what."

She spits into the sink.

"That's what I think of you and your lies. Your mom just said what Gran said. You know what she told me? She said you were making the whole thing up, that I shouldn't listen to you. I asked her all about 'hogwash.' 'Hogwash' isn't a secret code at all, is it?" She gargles noisily and then spits out again. "So you're just a liar, aren't you? Just a terrible liar." And she starts chanting at me, "Liar, liar, pants on fire. Nose is as long as a telephone wire! Liar, liar . . ." And now she's not just chanting, she's tap-dancing around the bathroom. Tap-dancing little toad.

All right, I'm

thinking, maybe this is a setback, but it's not a disaster. Just take it easy, play it cool. "Mom *would* say that, wouldn't she?" I tell her. "She doesn't want you worrying, that's all. You think what you like. You asked for proof, right?"

"Yes."

"Well, you're going to get it; and when you do, then you'll have to believe me, won't you? It could be tonight, you never know." Suddenly, Geraldine's not dancing anymore. I've got her worried again. "You've got toothpaste on your chin," I say, and I leave her standing there in the bathroom, her toothpasty mouth wide open and gaping after me.

It's later that night. I'm lying in the darkness waiting for Mom and Gran and Geraldine to go to sleep. It's been a long wait, but at last I hear Mom's radio go off. Gran's already snoring next door, and across the room Geraldine's breathing deeply and regularly — she has been for a while.

It's time. I get up. I don't make a sound. I tiptoe out of the room, the pepper shaker in my hand. As quietly as I can, I sneak around the house, sprinkling it everywhere — down the stairs and in the hallway, till there's no more pepper left.

I go back upstairs, trying hard not to

sneeze, slip into my bedroom, and shake Geraldine awake.

"I can smell him." I'm whispering and sniffing the air. "It smells peppery. Can you smell it? And it's cold and damp, too. He's been here, right in this room. I can feel it." She's sniffing, too, and then she's sitting straight up in bed. She's scared stiff.

"Pepper," she breathes. "It's pepper."

"Told you so, didn't I? Come on," I tell her. "I'll show you. He's probably back in the shed by now."

I put on my robe and slippers, but Geraldine's still just sitting there. I can see the whites of her eyes in the dark. "What's the matter?" I ask her.

"Nothing," she says.

"You're not scared, are you?"

"Of course not."

"It's all right," I tell her, ever so nicely, ever so kindly. "He's harmless. He's never hurt anyone, not so far, anyway."

She thinks about it for a few minutes. "I know it's just a trick," she says. "It must be. He's not real, he can't be. Your mom said. Gran said."

"Only one way to find out," I tell her. "Are you coming or not?"

She takes a while putting on her robe, but at last the two of us are creeping down the stairs. The wind is rattling the bathroom window and whining down the chimney. The floorboards are creaking under our feet. It's perfect. The kitchen door even groans on its hinges as I open it. It's all just like it should be, just like a real horror movie. For some reason, Geraldine doesn't seem to want to go any farther. I take her gently by the hand, and I feel her holding on tight.

"It's all right," I tell her. "It's all right."

Across the yard, I can see the dark, looming shape of the shed. "He's in there?" whispers Geraldine. "He's really in there?"

"Probably," I say. "Come on."

And so, still clutching my hand, she comes with me, tiptoeing across the lawn, her grip tightening with every step. Then we start running. Breathless, we reach the shed and crouch down under the window ledge.

I close my eyes and hope hard. Then, squeezing her hand, we both stand up slowly, inch by inch, and peer through the window.

For several minutes, there's nothing

but darkness in there, just blackness; and I'm thinking something must have gone wrong.

Then suddenly, it happens, exactly as I'd hoped. Two red eyes are glowing at us from the back of the shed. On. Off. On. Off. And then, somewhere close by, an owl hoots, the echoes of it filling the night sky. Fantastic, just fantastic. I couldn't have arranged it better.

Toowoo
Toowoo Woo Woo
Toowoo

Geraldine's hand is suddenly not gripping mine anymore. I look around, and there she is, stretched out on the grass at my feet. She's fainted! And I'm thinking: *She can't do that. She's not supposed to do that. That's not part of my grand plan at all!*

CHAPTER SEVEN
Rubber Duck

Now I'm really panicking. What am I going to do? I can't call for help, can I? Not after what I've done. I look around and see the goldfish pond. That gives me an idea. I scoop up handfuls of water, carry it back, and splash it all over Geraldine's face until, at last, she opens her eyes.

At the same moment, we hear this strange, unearthly voice, and it's coming from the inside of the shed.

"Come in. Come in. Is anyone out there? Come in. Come in."

Then there's something scratching
at the door, trying to claw its way out,
and it's shrieking and howling. The
blood goes cold in my veins.
Geraldine screams. I scream. We're
both clutching each other and

screaming our heads off, but the
scratching goes on and the howling
and that horrible voice telling us to
come in. "I know you're out there.
Come in. I know you're out there."
And then the owl's hooting again.

TooWoo TooWoo Woo Woo TooWoo

The ghost keeps calling us and howling, and he's still clawing at the door, and the door's shaking and rattling in its frame. I want to get up and run, but I can't. I can't move. I'm frozen where I am. All I can do is scream like Geraldine, only louder, so I don't have to hear the ghost's deathly voice and his bloodcurdling shrieks.

Suddenly, the lights in the house go on, then every light on the street. Then Mom and Gran are running toward us across the yard in their nightgowns.

"The red-eyed ghost!" Geraldine sobs. "He's in there, in the shed. I've seen him. I've *heard* him."

They look at us as if we're crazy.

"It's true," I
tell them. "The
ghost, he's
coming to get
us. He's clawing
his way out."
I'm crying, too.
I can't stop
myself.
Then Gran's hugging us close,
while Mom walks over to Dad's shed
and peers in through the window.
"Come in." The same voice again, but
louder. "Come in. This is Rubber
Duck, Rubber Duck, calling
Armadillo. Are you there, Armadillo?
Are you there? Come in, please. This
is Rubber Duck, Rubber Duck."

"That's no ghost," Mom says.
"That's your dad's CB radio, his toy.

He's got friends who call him up from all over the world. Rubber Duck's one of them, I guess. They always give themselves funny names."

Then there's more scratching at the door and more howling. Mom goes around and fishes for the key in the conch shell. She opens the door. You've guessed it. Out comes Bingo, yowling and barking and whimpering all at the same time. I'd locked him in by mistake.

Geraldine's not sobbing anymore, and neither am I. I'm kicking myself instead. I should have known. It should have been obvious. Why didn't

I think of it? How could I have been so stupid?

Mom's coming back toward us, toward me, Bingo jumping up around her. I'm in deep trouble. I know it. And there's nothing I can do about it.

"Well, Millie," she says, and there are dark clouds moving past the moon above her head, "you've been up to something, haven't you? All this red-eyed ghost nonsense, all this hogwash stuff. It's one of your little games, isn't it? Your dad would never leave his CB radio on. Never. No, someone's been in there and turned it on, hasn't she? That's how Bingo got himself locked in there, isn't it? Well, I didn't do it. Gran didn't do it. Geraldine certainly didn't do it. And neither did Bingo, I think. That leaves just you."

There's no point in denying it.
Gran's not hugging me anymore. She's
still hugging Geraldine, though, and
Geraldine's hugging her back. There's
a huge smile on her face. Little toad.

"I think we'd better have a talk,
Millie," she says. "Inside, in the
kitchen."

Things are not looking good.

CHAPTER EIGHT
Life's Funny Sometimes

Inside, Mom sits me down at the kitchen table where we have all our arguments and heart-to-heart chats. I don't like to look at her when she's angry. So I look down at my hands instead.

Well?

And so I tell her the whole
thing — it's the only way — from
beginning to end. How I don't like
Geraldine coming to stay, why I don't
like Geraldine, my grand plan, and
how it had all gone wrong.

She likes the part where I scared
myself silly — I can tell — but it's the
only part she does like. She's sighing
at me meaningfully.

"You haven't been very nice to Geraldine, have you?" she says.

There's that "nice" word again.

"No."

"I'll tell you what," she says. "I'll make you a deal. I won't tell your dad about any of this or about your going into his shed, but in return you've got to do something for me."

"What?"

"You've got to be nice to Geraldine. She's not that bad, and anyway, she's your cousin. So from now on, just be nice. And I mean *very* nice. Well?"

"All right," I tell her. I haven't got much of a choice, have I?

"And you can start by saying you're sorry to her right now."

I go up the stairs very

slowly. I am not looking forward to this, not one bit. I open the bedroom door. It's dark in there. I take a deep breath, and then I just go in and say it. "I'm sorry, Geraldine." She doesn't say anything. So I try again. "I said I'm sorry, Geraldine. I'm sorry if I frightened you."

That's when the wardrobe door

opens and there's this white shape floating silently across the room.

"Ahhh!" I scream.

Then the light goes on. Geraldine's

standing there and she's pulling the sheet off her head. She's smiling at me. "Only me," she says, ever so sweetly.

"You're a toad, a real little toad."

"Takes one to know one," she says. And then she's laughing and I'm laughing, and Bingo's there bouncing up and down, barking his head off.

We've been best friends ever since — all three of us. Life's funny sometimes, isn't it?